ig
the
Pig

A flip-the-page
RHYME & READ book

Colin and Jacqui Hawkins

Pat
&
Pals

patandpals.com

Do you know Mig the pig?

Mig the pig is very big.

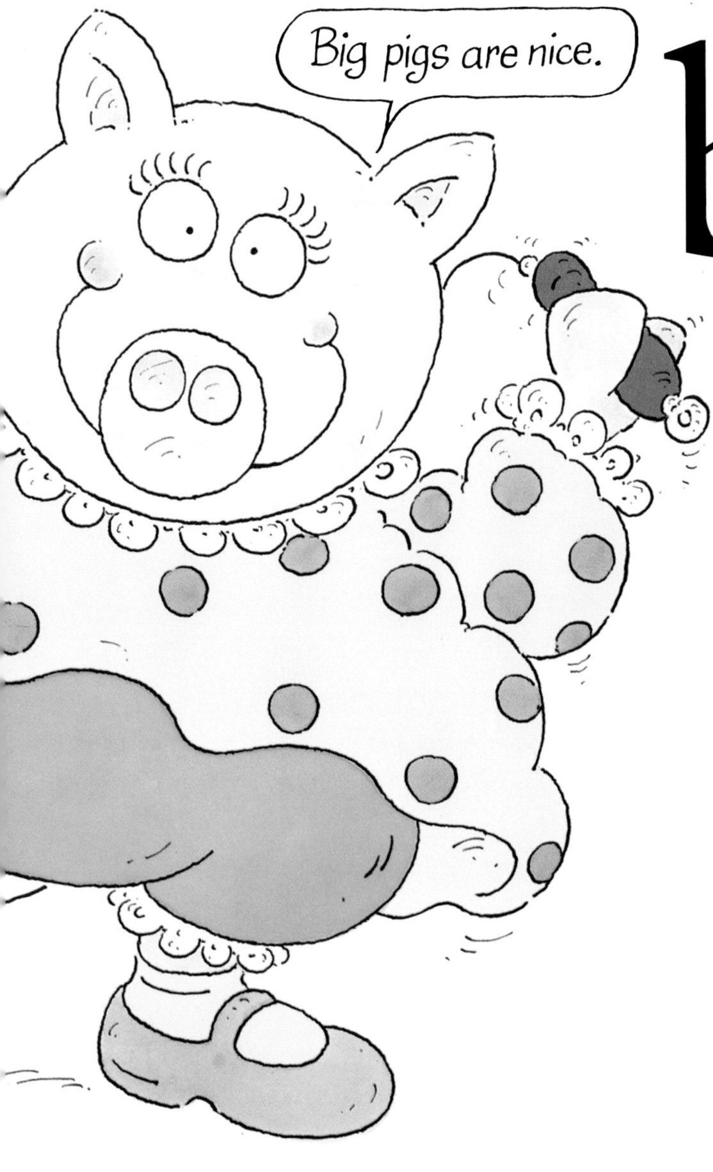

b

She likes to wear a bright red wig.

W

Mig often goes riding in her gig.

One day while out in her gig,
Mig stopped for a dig.

But the wind blew her red wig
onto a twig.

Oh dear!
Oh dear!
It's windy
here!

Mig shook the twig and down came her wig, along with a fig.

Now she has a wig...

...and a fig.

So happy was Mig to get back
her red wig, along with
a fig, that she danced
a wild jig.

What will Mig... ...do with her fig?

Then home in the gig to bake
the fig went the pig called Mig

Mig

Published in the United Kingdom in 2006
by Pat and Pals Limited,
15 Friars Stile Road,
London TW10 6NH

10 9 8 7 6 5 4 3 2 1

A CIP catalogue record for this book is available from the British Library

ISBN 1-905969-02-3

Printed in China by Imago Publishing Ltd

patandpals.com